RURAL TALES

A collection of dark,
fantasy short stories

Eoin Leydon O Connor

Eoin Leydon O Connor

CONTENTS

DYING BREEDS

The livestock began dying in late October. Here on our farm, in the west, we were never ready for such a thing. Oh sure, we'd had animals die before. Sheep, pigs, cows, the occasional hen snatched by the fox, that sort of thing But nothing ever like this. My childhood had been filled with grunting pigs, noisy sheep, my father bringing me out to show me how to milk the cows and teaching me to be extremely careful around the hazardous machinery. My uncle Tomas had lost seven of his fingers learning that the hard way, and two of my cousins died in a slurry pit. Despite all the joyous times I'd had, holding the spring lambs, scratching the newly born piglets and grooming the horses when they'd arrived, Dad never let me forget about the dangers that we encountered every day. And most importantly, that I should never get too attached to the animals, or name them, because it would upset me when we had to sell or kill them in the end.

Over the years, through childhood and into adolescence, I'd cried when we sold the piglets, or when Dad had to put the runt down because the sow couldn't feed it, or when we had to have one of our horses put down after they'd broken a leg. Once, I'd seen a murder of crows attack one of our spring lambs in the field next to our house and ran out to chase them away, crouching to steady the stumbling animal only to discover that the birds had pecked its eyes out. And after all of this, I'd assumed that I'd seen everything there was to see. That nothing on the farm could ever upset or frighten me ever again.

I was wrong.

I went out that morning as usual to feed the animals, expecting to hear them bleating or squeal as I approached the barn. But when I pushed open the door to go inside, I was met by complete and utter silence. I knew immediately that something was wrong. The horses usually have their heads over their pen gate, ready for me to pet them, but instead I found them lying on their sides, glassy-eyed and stiff. The pigs were the same - clumped together like they were sleeping - their eyes closed, their ears tucked down. The sheep in the pen next to them were like a large piece of fluff, lying on top of each other, a leg here and there, sticking out of the mass of white. Terrified by the sight, and not knowing what to do, I ran back towards the house.

Dad didn't know whether to yell or cry or just sit down and let it hit him. He checked every single one of the animals to make sure they were dead, then he called the vet. When you live in a small village everyone knows each other, whether you like it or not. Word would soon get out about the dead animals and questions would be asked. What do you think happened? You think he killed them? Was he careless in his practice? Did he poison them?

According to the vet, Rory – a local man and a family friend for years - it wasn't poison. Or anything they had eaten. It wasn't heart attacks or health related issues. In fact, Rory couldn't find anything whatsoever wrong with the animals other than that they were dead. Mum asked me to boil the kettle to make tea for Rory, but I hovered outside the dining room door, listening to what he was telling them.

'You're certain you found nothing wrong with them?' Dad asked.

'I'm positive Frank. I've checked every single one. They were all healthy as a horse. No trace of anything in their systems, no signs of diseases or organ failure, no signs of electrocution. It was like they just … dropped dead suddenly.'

'Animals don't all just 'drop dead' Rory. You know that as well as I do. Probably better. I'd be more inclined to believe you if it was just one of my sheep or pigs, but this is every animal in my farmyard wiped out. How am I supposed to explain this to the Department inspector?'

'At least there's nothing to suggest foul play.' Rory said.

Dad sighed loudly. 'I don't know. Fuck.'

Rory was right, we could take comfort at least that there was nothing malicious in these deaths and nothing to incriminate Dad.

And he wouldn't be the only one to have his livestock wiped out. Mr McGuinness, one of my old teachers from school, reared turkeys in his front garden that he sold at Christmas every year for a reasonable price. Sometimes Dad would buy one, but not this year. One Monday morning, before going to work, Mr McGuinness went outside to find feathers swirling in the wind around his front garden and in the coop where he kept the birds. All of them were dead. And just like the animals on our farm, Rory couldn't find a thing wrong with them.

This is when the panic began to set in across the village and people began bringing their pets to the vets to have them checked. Dogs, cats, parrots, hamsters, rats and mice. Not that Rory minded, he was getting a lot of business out of it. And people were genuinely scared. I would be too, if I had any animals left alive to bring to the vet.

After the deaths on our farm and the incident with Mr McGuinness's turkeys, things seemed to calm down for a while. Dad got a new shipment of animals, which were scheduled to arrive the following week. The farm had to be inspected and meet the requirements for Dad to properly keep the animals. Fortunately for him, we passed with flying colours. Mum and I drove the green truck into town about two miles away to get bags of feed for the new arrivals. Queuing up at the checkout with the shopping trolley full, I could feel everyone around staring at us when they thought I wasn't looking. And honestly, I didn't blame them. They probably had their suspicions. I felt a little better that Mr McGuinness's turkeys had died because at least we weren't the only ones it had happened to.

On the way back home, I sat in the front passenger seat beside Mum while she drove silently with the radio playing. As we drove across the bridge, we paused behind a red jeep that had stopped at the traffic lights. I gazed out the window at the river, leaning my temple against the glass and closing my eyes, listening to the rumble of the engine.

Something smacked against the windscreen of the truck, making Mum scream. A seagull, with speckled feathers, had dropped onto the glass, creating a jagged crack. Its head twisted ninety degrees, eyes open and staring in at us, its feathers blowing in the wind, several blowing away while its neck bled down onto the bonnet of the truck.

Our vehicle wasn't the only one hit. The red jeep in front of us honked its horn loudly, the driver's door opening and a woman jumped out, hands up to her face, crying and screaming. Something fell onto her head then, making her collapse and thrash around. A dead crow. A dull thump hit our roof and a parked car nearby suddenly blared to life as a fallen bird set its alarm off. On the pavement and tarmac, crows, seagulls, jackdaws, sparrows and a hawk collapsed, some on their back with their talons in the air. Mum told me to stay in the truck while she got out to look up at the sky, but I was too curious, and too full of fear to sit still. Up in the heavens, through the clouds and out of the sunlight, like small bombs, the birds fell, already dead by the time they'd hit the ground all around us. One of the seagulls splattered against the bonnet of the car next to us, flicking me with blood. In front of me, all through the queue of traffic leading up to the lights and beyond, littering the road, were the corpses of birds, with more falling across the roofs of the town like rain in the distance.

It didn't stop there. Rory was inundated with calls from people in hysterics over their pets that had died in the middle of the day. One of Mum's friends, Allison, returned home from work and opened the back door to call her dog Otto, only to find him lying against the fence at the back of the garden, his tongue lolling out of one side of his mouth.

There were other instances of people going into town to the kennels to retrieve their dogs and finding them dead too. Later, I found a stray cat under a bush covered with flies and bluebottles, buzzing loudly and crawling across its face and eyes, in and out of its open mouth, nestling in its dishevelled fur.

And then there was the first human death. Mr McCarthy, an elderly man, dropped dead in the shopping centre. I went to school with his grandson, Michael. As you can imagine, panic ensued, worse than before. That it had only been animals so far and not people provided some kind of safe barrier between us and them. This incident contradicted that assumption. According to his family, however, Mr McCarthy had a history of heart disease. That seemed to restore some normality. But the suspicion was still there, brewing amongst everyone.

It hasn't gotten any worse since then.

And now it's just us at home, surrounded by empty sheds and fields, the wind whispering through the trees and bushes. The lack of bird song, the absence of sheep bleating, animal grunting and neighing - the death of any sounds of life on the farm - makes it worse. Dad is in a state, waiting for the new horses to arrive tomorrow. I think he's scared that when they arrive, they'll drop dead too. And honestly, I don't blame him. It's in everyone's mind. On the nine o'clock news last night there were reporters standing in front of our post office, talking about how the Department of Agriculture inspectors were coming here to investigate all the incidents over the past week to try and determine the cause of it all. There is talk of the village being quarantined at some point but quarantined for what exactly, they don't know.

I get up and go into the kitchen to see Dad asleep in his armchair in the sitting room. Mum gently lays a blanket over his legs, careful so as not to wake him. She catches my eye as she turns around and puts a finger to her lips, closing the door and coming out to hug me.

'Is he okay?' I whisper.

'He's just tired. He hasn't slept since last week. He pretends to be asleep, so I won't annoy him. I've tried getting him to take something to help him nod off, but he insists he's fine.'

'What are we going to do with the new horses?' I ask.

'I don't know, Ciaran. I suppose we'll put them in the barn for the night. Wait and see what happens.' She shifts uneasily as she says this, dusting off her apron and going over to the sink to wash the vegetables for dinner. I go out the back door and down the porch steps, crossing the garden around the side of the house towards the field. Looking up, I see the empty sky with white clouds blowing over my head. Beyond the wall, in the field directly in front of me, is the wilting yellow grass, short this time of year. Silence presses in on all sides, and dotted across the entire field, are a murder of crows, every last one of them dead.

GLASS TEETH

The hospital was massive and all glass when I looked at it for the first time. The sheer size of the floor to ceiling windows and rooms was breath-taking. In the main lobby, a piano played itself, eerily. Apart from the soft melody that drifted around the otherwise wide white space, my shoes on the marble floor was the only other sound. The receptionist, donning the same white uniform with the green name tag that displayed her name 'Diane' looked up pleasantly at me. She smiled when she saw the bouquet of flowers I was carrying.

'You shouldn't have.' She said, taking them from me to inspect them. The man in the office next door, wearing a security uniform came out, snapping on the blue gloves and putting the flowers on the tray to be scanned under the blue lit machine. As a precaution, I understood why they needed to check. For health and safety reasons. I stood back and folded my arms, taking in the vast space around me. The lobby counter curved around the wall in the room, glimmering in the light that came in through the windows. A wide, spiral staircase rose to take you from floor to floor and next to them, the lifts. Couches, as white as everything else lay before the windows, giving you a magnificent view of the river spilling over the rocks and rushing away into the dipping valley below the hospital. Two horses galloped across the field on the other side of the river away into the hills where the sun perched on top, getting ready to say goodbye for the night. The sky outside was stained orange this evening, giving a true summer vibe to everything. From the rotating doors through which I'd entered, the breeze carried the sound of an ice-cream truck playing its song as it traversed the suburbs.

'Okay, we're all good to go.' Diane said, handing me back the flowers. 'He'll love them. They'll put a smile on his face.'

'I hope so.' I said. I decided to take the stairs to the first floor, beginning my trek down the long and wide corridor to Matthew's room. I passed by a set of windows that overlooked the main road and, in the distance, the town coming to life at night.

His door was ajar when I arrived, heart beating fast, palms sweaty against the crackling plastic wrapped around the flowers. I knocked three times and waited. Inside, I heard his chair squeak as he turned towards the noise. 'Come in.' He said. When I pushed back the door, he was sitting in his white t-shirt and tracksuit bottoms. He smirked when he saw me, slouched in the chair by the computer. He dropped his hands off the desk and into his lap, turning the chair towards me.

'Good evening.' I said, in an attempt to break the silence.

'Come in, Brad.' He said quietly.

'Happy Birthday.' I said, holding out the bouquet. He rose to take them, smelling them and smirked again, keeping his lips tight like he always did. I took in his figure while he went to fetch a vase from his little kitchen adjacent to his living quarters. Tall, broad shoulders, with sandy coloured hair that always looks messy, falling into his eyes. He reached up to take a vase from the top shelf of the kitchen units no problem, a feat that would require me to get a small ladder to do. He filled the vase at the sink and placed them on the table in the corner of the room, beside a small box. Outside, the sun was setting fast, dimming the light around us with each passing second. He stared at me in the growing darkness, eyes twinkling with an air of something I wasn't quite familiar with.

'So, how does it feel, being twenty-one?'

He shrugged. 'Practically the same as being twenty. Do I look older?'

'Only in the best of ways.' I said, trying to keep my breathing steady. I hoped that he couldn't see through my calm façade to the nerves gnawing away at my insides.

'Well, sit down. Would you like to sit down?' He asked, running a hand through his long hair.

'Why don't you get that mop cut?' I teased, reaching up to touch his head with clammy hands. The hair tangling in between my fingers for a moment, making his eyes water. He shook his head, now so close to me that I could smell his breath. I wanted to kiss him, but he stepped back and put his hands in his pockets.

'Why don't we get you a haircut?' I said, more as an excuse for us to do something rather than realising it was a good idea.

'Sure.' He said, dropping his eyes to the floor for a moment before taking a step towards the door. I reached out to take his hand, but he kept his in the tracksuit bottoms, looking straight ahead. Feeling a little wounded, I kept mine by my sides as we strolled silently down towards the shops at the other end of the hospital.

Brightly lit signs above the shutters read Spar and Barry's Barber among several others. An Eason's shop with stationery and best-selling books was practically empty apart from two patients browsing. Matthew went in through the open door to the barber's. A small space with three chairs in front of mirrors, a counter with a cash register and a three-seater couch, red walls, posters of hair models, a green cactus plant in the corner and a smell of aftershave and shaving cream lingering in the air.

'Hello boys.' The barber looked up from behind the counter on his phone. A good-looking man with an eastern European look to him, though he spoke fluent English. He wore tight black jeans revealing the shape of his wallet and phone in his pockets, black shoes with thick white socks and a tight shirt that clung to his muscular figure. His jet-black hair was shaved tightly at the sides and gelled on top. He was delicious looking, in short. But then again, barber boys are always like that. I sat down on the three-seater and looked at Matthew, trying my best to smile.

'The usual.' He said, barely moving his lips. Taking the chair that made it so I couldn't see his face in the reflection of the glass, I ended up staring at the back of the barber while he snipped Matthew's hair. I sat there, taking off my jacket, crossing my legs. A small lump had formed in my throat, and I tried my best not to pout. This was his birthday after all. We were supposed to be celebrating, but right now, I wasn't so sure. He didn't seem all that interested in being with me. Was I doing something wrong? Had I offended him by bringing him those flowers?

No. I was pretty sure, from the second I knocked on his door, he had twisted around in his seat expecting someone else to walk in. Maybe his parents. Or maybe Diane from reception.

Or maybe you're just reading too much into it and you need to stop overthinking it for fuck's sake.

My brain was right. I *was* overthinking it. This wasn't my problem. I was doing everything right.

Maybe he just didn't want to have his hair cut. Well then why didn't he just say no? He had no problem saying it last week when I offered to take him out to dinner. I just wasn't aware that he wasn't allowed to leave the hospital. This whole dating another guy thing was still pretty new for both of us. We had only been on one date before this. And the reason being was because our parents had set it up. It was like having a playdate as a child. It felt so patronising at first, but once I'd seen Matthew's face, I'd forgotten about my resentment. Shallow, I know. Never judge a book by its cover. Well, I think I was beginning to appreciate that statement a little more after tonight's visit. He might be handsome and cute to me, but there were clearly issues underneath that. Issues he obviously didn't feel like sharing.

And honestly, that wasn't a bad thing. Maybe he was just shy. Maybe I intimidated him, or he didn't like me that much. Maybe we just had no chemistry. A simple fact that we'd have to face up to soon.

'I'm just popping next door to the shop.' I announced, standing up. He didn't answer and I left with the lump in my throat feeling very hard to swallow. This was hurtful. Not only was he distant, but now he was blatantly ignoring me. I browsed through Spar before I bought a packet of Wine Gums and put them in my coat pocket while I waited for the barber to finish.

I stood up and paid for it before Matthew could, hoping that my actions would inspire some interest in the situation. Maybe even a 'Thank you'. But no, when we finished, Matthew just nodded towards the barber, who winked back knowingly, making my blood boil. I was grinding my teeth while I counted to ten in my head and opened the packet of Wine Gums to offer Matthew one. He winked at me, leaning in abruptly to kiss my cheek as he took a handful and slipped them quickly into his mouth.

Okay, now I was confused. What the hell was he playing at? He winks at me, after ignoring me and acting all distant and uninterested. We walked back up towards his room, slowly, the only sound being our footsteps and the crackle of the packet of Wine Gums as we reached in to take them out. I handed him the rest, feeling sickly sluggish after eating so much. He said nothing as we entered his room and I looked at him, taking in his face for the first time since his hair had been shortened.

Actually, it looked good. Shorter and a little spikier, it made him look younger. If I had to guess his age, I would think he was the same age as me. For just a second, I forgot about my anger and smiled and then, unexpectedly, he did the same. His lips parted and I saw a wet glimmer of his teeth, shining and … clear.

My smile faltered. He suddenly sealed his mouth and rubbed a hand over his lips, dropping his gaze again.

'You're beautiful.' I said abruptly, making him look

up at me. The moment I said it, I almost regretted it. He looked like he wanted to say something too but decided against it. 'Thanks.' Was all he said, looking down to the floor again, going over to the window. The outside world had darkened and now the stars were beginning to show, coming through the navy-blue haze above us in the heavens. He kept his hands in his pockets as he watched them. I stood beside him and reached down to take his hand, making him tense a little. Pulling his hand out of his pocket, linking my fingers through his, they were warm and clammy compared to mine which were icy and sticky from the sweets. In the silence, we stood, each probably just as tense as the other.

'Are you alright?' I asked.

'Yeah. Fine.' He said, just barely above a whisper.

'You don't look fine.'

'I am. I promise.'

'Look me in the eye and tell me that.'

He glanced at me then, wetting his lips and opened his mouth slowly, taking a deep breath. 'I am fine.' He said again, flashing his teeth, the glimmer coming through again, letting me see them. I blinked.

'Can I be honest with you?' He whispered.

I nodded my head. 'Of course. Always.' I felt weird saying it, like I was assuring him he could trust someone he barely knew. But I wanted him to know that regardless. When I smiled at him, he did the same, his lips pulling back over his teeth, showing me the crystal-clear incisors and canines. I knew it. I thought I'd peaked a glance at them just a moment earlier, but now, I was sure. I reached up and leaned in towards his mouth, to which he hesitated before smiling at me again, wider this time. Relieved probably, because of my reaction. I hadn't screamed or freaked out. Quite the opposite actually. I was fascinated by this. The room was dark, so I leaned down to switch on the lamp, casting yellow light on his glass teeth.

He opened his mouth for me, allowing me to see right into his gums, the molars and premolars like diamonds, shaped exactly like normal teeth, nothing bizarre about them other than the material they were composed from. Even at the back, where the tips of new wisdom teeth were pushing through, complete with little colourful glistening pieces of wine gums that had gotten stuck in them amazed me, to the point where I let out a laugh. He laughed too, taking my hands eagerly and in that moment, so close together, I had an epiphany. It all made sense now, his behaviour and attitude, coming into perspective. And I was so overjoyed by the relief that I was wrong about him, that I leaned in and kissed him right on the mouth. His lips were soft and fuller than I'd expected, a little bit of stubble rubbed against my upper lip, but he tasted sweet from the wine gums. He kissed me back, putting his palms to my face, around the back of my head, down to the base of my neck and then trailed it down my back. I even went as far as to slip my tongue into his mouth. A bold move, but I did it anyway and he didn't pull away.

It was like a normal kiss, but the clink of our teeth touching was smooth. When I pulled away I reached up gently with the tip of my index finger to touch his front teeth. He didn't seem to mind so I traced it along the bottom row in along the sharp canines, the ones at the back, all around his mouth. His lips closed around my fingers, warming them before I pulled them out.

'They're fascinating. Are they real glass?'

'Yes. All of them.'

How come you didn't tell me sooner?'

'I was scared you'd hate me because of it.' He said, swallowing hard, his Adam's apple bobbing.

'No, of course not. How could I hate you for that? Just because you've got glass teeth?'

He laughed then, tears in his eyes, shimmering before spilling down his cheeks. I wiped them away with my sleeve.

'I want to show you something.' He turned and walked over to the table he'd put the vase with the flowers on earlier. He picked up the little rectangular box on clawed feet, embedded with a gold design on top of a lion's head. He brought it over to me and opened it, revealing a black cushioned surface with two lines of baby glass teeth, arranged neatly.

'Wow.' I said.

'Take one.' He said, smiling again, proudly showing his features now. 'I'd like you to have one.'

'Me? Why? They're your teeth.'

'Because I'd like you to. That way you'll have a little piece of me with you when you go home. You're the first person I've ever shown. Apart from my Mum and Dad that is.'

When he said that I felt a rush of affection for him, an urge to throw my arms around him but I restrained myself. That twinkle in his eyes was back and now I understood why this time. Reaching into the box, I took one of the small molar teeth, laying it out in the flat of my palm, watching the light wink off it.

'Thank you. I'll put it with my Waterford crystal collection when I go home.' That made him laugh, flashing his teeth in full display, unafraid that I would see them. And in that light, he was amazing in front of me. I crossed to him and wrapped my arms around him, hugging him tightly, closing my eyes. He hugged me back immediately and we stood there for a little while. 'Happy Birthday.' I whispered to him, low in his ear and felt his hug tighten on me.

When I had said my goodbyes, I walked back down

the corridor and descended the spiral stairs to the ground floor lobby, waving goodnight to Diane who winked knowingly at me on my way out and told me to take care of myself. I walked home in the dark, turning and casting a glance at the hospital, lit brightly against the darkness pressing in on all sides. In the silence of the night, I smiled all the way home, feeling like the tooth in my pocket was glowing brightly while I walked. When I arrived, Mum and Dad were watching television, so I went straight in to show them the tooth.

'Mum look what Matthew gave me.' I said, not worrying what she would think because she probably wouldn't assume it's from his mouth.

'He gave you a souvenir. How nice.' She said, smiling at the tooth in my hand. Dad smiled too, but neither one of them understood and I was okay with that.

'Is it okay if I put it in with the whiskey glasses?'

'Of course.' She said, probably finding it humorous. I went into the dining room to my grandmother's antique cabinet that she gifted to Dad when she passed away. I placed the tooth in with the Waterford Collection of whiskey glasses that come out once in a blue moon for birthday parties or Christmas or whatever the celebration might be. Beside the glasses with their engravings and designs, it looked kind of cute. I closed the cabinet, admiring it for a moment longer before I retired upstairs to bed.

DEVILISHLY

On the couch in his sitting room, I tremble with nerves while he fetches glasses from the kitchen. When I walked in, he had the fire lit. It was already blazing in the hearth, warming the entire room and fogging up my glasses from the sudden contrast to the freezing weather outside. He seems so at ease with himself, in the comforts of his own home, in the presence of his newly wed husband. I stare down at the wedding ring on my finger. It feels heavier than it should be, but that's probably in my head. My mind has been racing all night, from the walk to the shop to buy the steaks he asked me to bring and then over to his house ... our house now. I hear him throwing the steaks into the pan in the kitchen and I can't help but admire him. The fact that he's so calm and cool as always and handsome and *mine*.

That last statement makes me smile. I stare at the flames. I am warm enough to take off my jumper and wipe the drizzle off my forehead from where the snowflakes melted into my hair and ran down my temples. Kieran starts to whistle in the kitchen, cooking to his heart's content. I stand up to stretch.

'Thomas.' he calls. I hear the glasses clink in his hands as he picks them up, bringing them in to me. He has donned the white apron. He stands there, dressed in his black formal silk shirt with the top three buttons undone, the press pants and black pointy shoes. He could be going to a funeral if not for the apron. His nose and jaw, so sharp and perfectly edged, make my stomach churn with butterflies. He smiles warmly.

'A toast, pet.' he lays the glasses down and takes the corkscrew out of his pocket to pop the champagne, pouring it out with one hand behind his back and filling my glass first. We clink them together. 'To us.' he says.

'To us.' I repeat, taking a sip and keeping my eyes on him.

I let the champagne bubbles cut my throat as I swallow. He looks at me hungrily, licking his lips. 'Are you starving?' he asks, voice low.

'Yes.' Winking, he takes my hand and guides me into the kitchen to where steam rises off the steaks sizzling in the pan on the gas hob. Sirloin steaks, his favourite and specialty. He always cooks this for me on my birthday and at Christmas time. In the ten years that we've been dating, I've never grown tired of his meals. And he's never cooked one wrong. Never have I gotten food poisoning because of his culinary skills. And neither has he. In fact, he's never gotten sick from anything, remarkably.

I sit at the island in the centre of the kitchen with my bubbling golden glass and sip it quietly while he dances around the hob, adding a drop of red wine to the steaks, making flames snap up for a split second, lighting up his face and eyes in their glow. With a prong, he flips the meat, letting it sizzle and ladles a spoonful of sauce from another bubbling pot into a bowl and slides it onto the table for me. 'Here, try this baby.'

Tentatively, I blow on the sauce and sip it gently, allowing the flavours to spread across my taste buds and fill my pallet. 'Peppercorn.' I smile, making him wink. 'How *did* you know?'

'I know you like the back of my hand.' He says, returning to the pan. After a few minutes, he serves the steaks onto the plates and spreads the sauce across them, lighting the candle in the centre of the island and adding a dusting of garlic to the food. He watches me while I eat the meal, taking my hand in his warm one and rubbing my knuckles with his thumb. 'You like it?'

'It's delicious, as always.' I wink at him now. Satisfied, he cuts into his own dinner and for the next few minutes, we eat in content silence. Outside, in one of the other houses in the neighbourhood, someone plays the Cello and piano in a duet. The soft melody is carried in through the window. He lifts my hand and kisses it, drawing my attention back to him.

'I love you.' He whispers, a warm breath through my fingers and tickling my wrist. When we're finished eating, he loads up the dishwasher and pours out the rest of the champagne for us, draining his glass quicker than I do. Then he leans on the counter, reaching over to touch my face. His fingers sending static electricity across my skin, making my hair stand on end and my insides melt. Closing my eyes, I relax as I always do under his touch, letting his hand explore the shape of my skull, right down to the nape of my neck. Then he leans in and kisses me right on the mouth.

His kiss is as tender as the steaks. It burns with desires that I'm sure are racing through both our minds right now. In the heat of the moment, I reach out and take his forearms, pulling him closer to me. I grip his black shirt and he slides off the stool to stand, bent slightly forward to embrace me. He opens his mouth to kiss me again, but something presses against my forehead, sharp and pointy, like a toothpick, pushing against the skin. I moan, pulling back just as whatever it is breaks the skin and a sharp jab of pain registers. I push him away and reach up to touch my head just as two drops of blood well up and come away on my fingers. 'What the hell-' I say.

Protruding from his forehead, above each eye, like that of a bull, are two small horns. Just the tips coming through, but they're horns, nonetheless. He looks down, embarrassed before meeting my eyes again. 'It's okay.' he says, calmly. 'It's nothing to be scared of. C'mere, let me see.' He gently touches my forehead while I sit there in shock, then takes my head in both his hands and pulls me closer to press his tongue to the two small wounds. His tongue is burning hot, but I feel the holes close. When he lets me go, I reach up to touch my forehead and through the warm wetness of his saliva, I find the pricks have disappeared. He stares at me.

'What just happened?'

To that, he smiles and takes my hand again, bringing it up to the horns and letting me brush my fingers against them. They are sharp. Too sharp. But beautiful … despite the demonic appearance they give him, they are beautiful. If I were to drag my finger across the tip of one, it would slice it open, and I would bleed again. He closes his eyes as I explore his anomaly. The horns are made of bone, and they are warm. And real. One hundred percent real, growing out of his forehead.

'Who are you?' I ask. Kieran just smiles, a little sadly.

'I'm yours. It's okay, I know it's a shock, but it's okay. I'm not gonna hurt you. I promise.'

'Where did they come from?' I ask. In response, he squeezes his eyes shut, face contorted and before me, the horns pull back into the skin of his forehead, the holes they leave behind closing slowly until his forehead is back to normal, like it was a few moments ago. Then he smiles again, touching my wrist.

I get up, taking my hands back, and stand behind the stool, to put something between us.

'I'm going to bed.'

He doesn't try to stop me, just sits looking at me, unphased by my reaction. Before anything else can happen, I leave the kitchen and walk up the stairs to the bedroom that might as well be mine too at this stage. My mother was opposed to us moving in together until we got married and now that we finally have, she's at home packing my belongings away. I might just stop her tomorrow.

In the darkness of the bedroom, I gaze at his things. His photographs of his parents and sister. Photos of the two of us throughout the years and his school photos when he was a few years younger. His clothes are strung over the back of one of the chairs and on the floor. His bed, with fresh sheets, courtesy of me, invites me to lie in it. But at the same time, seems all the more sinister. I'm not sure about what I just witnessed downstairs, was it the champagne? Did I hallucinate? Am I just nuts? Or was it all real? I reach up and touch my forehead, where the skin has completely healed, but behind that, my skull throbs a little bit, reminding me that it was real.

With my mind racing and my heart in my mouth, I sit down on the bed and take a deep breath, then kick off my shoes and leave my glasses on the bedside table, pulling the duvet over me, still fully dressed. The bed sheets are cool and soft, the memory foam moulding around my figure. I close my eyes, images of those horns filling my head.

For a while, I lie there, unsure of what to do or think. Should I go back downstairs to him or should I leave? Should I just accept it? He has horns, so what? He's still the same man I married. He still has the exact same personality, he's still the human I fell in love with.

Is he? A dark corner of my mind has piped up.

How can you be so sure?

Because I would know, that's how. I know him better than anyone. And vice versa. Like he said, like the back of your hand. We've been together for over a decade and only now have I seen … what I just saw. How could he have kept that a secret from me this entire time?

Ah, I don't know. I'm overthinking things now. At this rate I'll never be able to get to sleep. With the steaks sitting in my stomach, I can't seem to rest. But when I think about going back downstairs, my gut fails me. I sit up and watch the door, waiting for him to come up to me. After what feels like an eternity, I lie back down and close my eyes again, sleep threatening to overcome me now. That's when I hear the footfalls on the stairs and the door opens.

I look up and see him standing there, in the doorway, silhouetted by the light in the hall. A long shadow stretches into the room and up onto the bed. Like something out of *Dracula*. He flicks the light off in the hallway and comes into the bedroom. The horns protruding from his head once more, his eyes seem to have darkened in colour. At the end of the bed, he unbuttons his shirt and throws it on the ground, then removes the rest of his clothes. When he pulls down his underpants, I see a tail. Long and spurting what seems to be hair, it falls down and sways from side to side. He comes towards me and climbs onto the bed, sliding between the sheets to wrap his arms around me and hold me close to him. One hand stroking the side of my face. In the warmth of his embrace, despite my instincts telling me to flee, my body relaxes under his touch as it always does, and my eyelids become droopy.

'Sleep.' he whispers to me.

In the next few moments, I slip away into unconsciousness. No dreams plague my mind, or nightmares either. I sleep right through the night.

When the winter blue morning light spills in through the open blinds, I rise from my slumber to find Kieran still asleep beside me, sound to the world. I slip quietly out of bed, the cold air of the house immediately grabbing me. Donning his bathrobe, I walk down the hall to the bathroom, splashing my face with water, the events of last night still horribly vivid in my mind. Leaning against the sink, I stare back at my reflection, pale-faced and sleepy-eyed. My hands are a little shaky, the ring on my left hand still weighing heavily. I take it off and lay it on the sink, not wanting to put it anywhere near my skin.

A wave of nausea suddenly comes over me, making me dizzy and having to grip the edge of the sink. After a moment, my head begins to throb, right where the horns punctured my skin and I double over, vomiting what's left of last night's meal down the drain. I continue until green bile comes up and all that's left is dry retching. When the moment passes, I wash my mouth out with water and reach for my ring, placing it back on my finger. The throbbing in my head ebbs away then. The nausea calming down, my stomach no longer churning and then … nothing at all. The ring still feels heavy, but other than that, I'm fine. Glancing at my reflection, I notice him, standing in the doorway behind me, silently watching, horns and everything still there. He approaches me and wraps his warm hands around me.

'Thomas, you're sick.'

'I'm okay now.' I say, washing the last bits of vomit down the drain.

'Was it the steaks? Did I not cook them right?'

'No, it's alright. Maybe I've caught a bug or something.'

'Come back to bed. If you lay down, you'll feel better.'

'I'll be right there. I promise. I just want to get a drink of water first.'

'I'll get it for you.' He says.

'No, I'll do it. I might go outside and get some fresh air too.'

He lets me go and watches as I leave the bathroom and go downstairs. When I reach the kitchen, I gulp down three glasses of water to wet my throat and soothe the burning in it. In the back garden, the birds have gathered at the feeders, chirping happily while they peck at the food in the nets. I open the back door and breathe in the fresh air from the winter morning. It *does* make me feel better. By the feeders, two robin redbreasts feed beside each other before taking off, flying back to their nest to their young ones. They say that robins mate for life. I will watch the birds for a little while longer, before I go back inside and upstairs to the bedroom where he is waiting for me.

THE BLOODLESS
AND MARIE

Marie pulled up beside Frank's house, making sure not to block the driveway. Although Frank was elderly and didn't drive anymore, hadn't done so for nearly five years now, he still disliked it when someone blocked his car. When she asked about it, Frank replied that if an emergency occurred and he had to drive himself to safety, he could escape with relative ease. To help calm his fear, Marie had gotten him one of those buttons to wear around his neck, so all he'd have to do is press it and the ambulance would be on its way. Frank didn't want to have to rely on an ambulance, he would have preferred to drive himself to the hospital. Marie had said it would put her mind at rest, knowing that he would be able to get a hold of the authorities himself, in case something happened in the middle of the night, and she was at home asleep and couldn't help him. The dread that spread through her stomach when she thought about how Frank might fall down the stairs and be lying in a heap at the bottom while she slept soundly nearly two miles away.

She brought his morning shopping with her, eggs and rashers, sausages, teabags and toilet paper like he'd asked for. It was barely half-eight when she'd pulled in and walked up the drive to the door. Frank was the very definition of an early bird. One thing he and Marie first bonded over was the fact that both of them were such anxious people they would never ever have a lie-in in the morning. When she'd first started coming to visit him as his new Home Help, he'd been very pleased to know that she was up at the crack of dawn like he was. That way, they wouldn't clash, what with her coming too late in the morning while he sat there waiting for his shopping. Despite Frank insisting that he didn't tolerate tardiness in any shape or form, Marie got the impression that underneath his hard exterior, he was simply lonely.

When she put the bags down to get her key and let herself in, she noticed something was wrong. Firstly, the house was silent and secondly it was cold. Frank was always awake at this time every morning, sitting in his dressing gown at the kitchen table doing the crossword. The house was always warm, the radio was always on. The spring morning light filtered in through the open blinds in the kitchen. If the blinds were open, that meant Frank was awake.

'Hello?' She called. 'Frank?' No answer. She put the bags down in the hall and went into the kitchen. The paper hadn't been touched and still had the elastic band around it. Marie stood there, silent.

She went up the stairs to his room and knocked on the door, pushed it open. The room was lit by the sun coming in through the window and the bed was made. A wave of dread came over her. She checked the bathroom and spare bedroom. She went back downstairs and into the sitting room.

Frank was in his armchair, fully dressed in his brown trousers and green jumper. His walking was stick leaning up against the arm of the chair, his hands joined and resting on his chest. His eyes were open.

'Frank.' She said, her own voice weak and small. She crossed the room to him, looking him straight in the eye. His white hair had been combed neatly. She reached out and touched his skin. He was stone cold.

One time, when she was in her forties, her sister took her to a wax museum for her birthday - much to Marie's dislike - mostly to creep her out. The figurines had unnerved her in a way she had never before experienced. For every wax statue they passed, she'd half-expected it to jump at her suddenly. But of course, they didn't. The one thing that creeped her out was the eyes, so real. Uncanny valley.

That was how she felt when she gazed at Frank, stiffly sitting in that armchair in his sitting room, cold as ice. The only other time she'd felt that coldness was when she touched her mother's hand in the casket at her funeral. But there was something else that frightened her about Frank. His skin was discoloured and wrinkled. It looked unnatural. She backed away from his corpse and went to get the phone.

The coroner came and took the body away. She'd waited in the kitchen, like they'd told her, not disturbing Frank until she'd heard the sirens and yanked the front door open, moving the shopping bags out of the way so that the paramedics wouldn't trip over them and pointed them towards the sitting room. She'd noticed that they'd paused before going in, no doubt just as shocked as she was upon seeing Frank, or at least, what was left of him.

When she had calmed down enough, one of the officers came to take her to the police station to ask her some questions. They were pretty simple. What was her connection to Frank? How long had she known him and worked as a Home Help? When was the last time she'd seen him alive? Did he have any other family? Did he have any enemies? Was there anyone who might want to do him harm? They also announced that Frank had died around midnight the previous night and where had Marie been at that time, and could anyone confirm that?

As far as she was concerned, she had been home alone, in bed at that time. But given the fact that she lived alone, her statement was suspect, at least to them. She couldn't care less what they thought. She would never, ever hurt Frank. The only thing that helped them believe her, was the fact that whoever had murdered Frank knew how to drain the blood out of the body without spilling one drop. Only someone who knew how to hunt would know that, and no offence to Marie, but she wasn't exactly in the pinnacle of her youth, so it was unlikely she had done it. When all was said and done, they had let her go home and said they would call if they had any further questions.

It was six weeks before they rang her to tell her they had the results of the autopsy. She wasn't allowed to be there in the room with them for the examination, but she waited outside the morgue.

A wave of nausea came over her as she sat, bending forward, hands on her knees. She was dreading when the coroner came out to tell her what had happened to Frank. Having never married, he didn't have any children or next of kin to identify his body. So of course, Marie had to fill that role. She heard the door to the morgue open and her stomach clenched.

'Marie O'Neill?' The coroner asked, dressed in blue clothes with gloves and a face mask on. She could only nod in response while he stood back to let her into the room. Frank's body was in one of those awful drawers against the far walls, all by himself. She knew that he wasn't really there, his soul was gone. It had passed on to that better place that she believed came after death, but still, it couldn't shake the overwhelming sense of dread and sickness that was threatening to make her collapse.

The coroner, a man named Nick, opened the drawer and showed her the body, pulling back the sheet to reveal Frank's face, his eyes closed now, the smirk still there. She almost laughed. Even in death, he was still just as smug as usual. She half-expected him to open his eyes when Nick wasn't looking and wink up at her. But of course, he did no such thing. She spotted the V-shaped stitched up wound in his chest, where Nick had cut him open. His skin was so pale, no red marks around where he had been sewn back up. She put one hand over her mouth and tried to remember how to breathe. Nick turned to her, taking the mask away from his face.

'What happened to him?' She said before Nick could say anything. He looked at her, understandingly. He'd probably seen all kinds of displays of grief in his career. Working as a mortician must be a horrible job, Marie thought.

'We're not exactly sure, but he's lost all his blood. Actually, it was removed. Someone drained his blood.'

'What do you mean 'drained his blood'? Who would do that?'

'I don't know, ma'am. But the cause of death was most-likely blood loss. Someone stuck a needle into him and took it all out.'

'Why?' She snapped.

He pressed his mouth into a thin line and regarded her professionally. 'I don't know.'

She looked down at Frank's body again, feeling the nausea coming back suddenly and turned to vomit onto the floor instead of Frank's corpse.

When she went home, the world felt like a very different place. Glancing out her kitchen window into the back garden, she watched the sun glisten off her wind chimes and greenhouse roof. But the picture was different to the sunny spring morning she'd witnessed weeks ago. Instead of a happy encounter with Frank, cooking him his breakfast and helping him figure out his crossword like she usually would, she'd witnessed a murderer's handywork. If the coroner was right, someone had broken into Frank's home while he'd slept upstairs and drained his blood without waking him up. Then, once they'd taken all ten pints, dressed the corpse and brushed its hair, carried it downstairs to the sitting room and positioned it in the armchair, with the walking stick beside it, for Marie to find.

And that was what scared her the most…

They had positioned Frank's body especially for Marie to find. Like they knew she would be coming the next morning. Thinking about that made her shiver. She filled a glass with water and sipped it slowly, not sure whether she should sit down or pace the kitchen. Maybe she should call her sister Alyssa to come over. She didn't feel like staying home alone.

And then, an awful thought came into her head. What if … the person who had murdered Frank and left him for her to find, knew where she lived? With that thought in mind, she clawed through her handbag to grab her phone. She dialled the number, but before she pressed the green button, second guessed herself and thought better of it. Perhaps she was just paranoid. After all, she lived in a nice part of town, and she always locked her doors and windows before she went to bed. Plus, in the event someone did break in, she had a security system. Maybe she should get herself one of those buttons she'd gotten Frank.

What little good it did him …

Upstairs, she opened the wardrobe door and took out the crowbar she kept in case of emergencies. It wasn't like she had a concealed weapon in the house. Crowbars were something you would find in people's homes all the time. And she was pretty sure she could crack someone's skull if they came at her in the middle of the night …

She left it beside the bed and went back downstairs to take two Panadol.

The police didn't call until Wednesday, to tell Marie that they had confirmed Frank's cause of death was blood loss and that they were treating it like a homicide. They hadn't found any evidence at the scene to help them in their leads and when she asked them if they had any suspects, they replied stiffly that they had not. In her best interests, she voiced her paranoia about the murderer knowing where she lived and to make her feel better, the police offered to put a car outside the house until they caught whoever it was, but she declined the offer. That might have done more bad than good in the long run and besides … she had her own ways of protecting herself (she threw a glance at the crowbar as she said that).

They buried Frank the following Thursday morning in the local town cemetery. Marie's sister accompanied her to the service where she went up on the altar to deliver the eulogy, speaking loudly and clearly to the nearly empty church. Despite knowing that the turnout would be poor, she still felt a little bit stung by the lack of attendants. Frank had been quite a proud, private man, but he was never a bad person, at least not to Marie. In the three years she'd been his Home Help, he'd always gotten on well with her, even going out of his way to give her a present on her birthday and Christmas. He'd served his duties being a university teacher in Oxford (a fact he was very proud of) and now that he was dead, nobody seemed to care or acknowledge his achievements in life, something that he'd taken the time to explain to Marie over their morning conversations while she cooked his breakfast. All the years he'd lived, all that he'd achieved, everything he'd done, all for no one to remember now that he was stone cold. And that really upset her. So much so that she deviated from what she'd written halfway through the eulogy and spoke, on a very personal note, about what kind of man Frank had been to her in the short time she'd known him.

'Frank Devereaux was an extremely proud and stubborn man all his life. I only knew Frank for three years, but, in that short time, I felt like he was more than just someone I went to work for every single day. He was my friend. And I think I was his as well. To me, Frank was someone I could confide in, I could talk to honestly. Because I felt like I could trust him and vice versa. As someone who loved his independence and individuality, he never married or settled down with anyone and I think in the last years of his life, he was quite lonely. As someone who's never done that either .... I think I recognised that in Frank, and I think that was one of the first things we bonded over. That and the fact that both of us were morning people and finding one of those is like searching for a needle in a haystack.' A murmur of laughter echoed in the church, setting her nerves at ease.

'But Frank was a loyal and trustworthy man, that I'm sure of and he didn't deserve to die the way he did. And I know that the police are out there as I say these words, searching for the person that ended Frank's life. And I know ... that they will find them, and they will bring justice to Frank Devereaux.'

The priest, Alyssa and a few other people listening seemed to drink in every word of hers, but she knew that it would go out of their heads as soon as they left the church. Alyssa took her by the arm and led her back outside after they removed the coffin from the altar and put it into the hearse. 'That was beautiful.' She'd said.

At the grave, when they'd filled it in, Marie stayed behind for several minutes, the wind cutting into her. She stood with her hands joined, staring at the tombstone with the oval photograph of Frank, taken by her on his previous birthday. The smirk on his face was identical to the one that his corpse was wearing when she'd found him. Tearing her eyes away from the grave, she walked down the path to where Alyssa leaned against the car, waiting for her. She hugged her tightly, telling her it would be okay before they got in and she drove Marie home.

Two weeks passed and they never got any closer to finding Frank's murderer. Marie got the impression that any day now, they would be calling her to tell her they were calling off the search. As distraught as she was, she couldn't let it show while she went back to work, calling in on her other Home Help patients. An elderly lady who lived across town named Rose had rung her the previous afternoon to ask her to bring over a bouquet of flowers the next day for her daughter's birthday. Marie told her she would be there first thing in the morning, to which

Rose replied that she only got up around ten o'clock so she should come around half ten or eleven if she wouldn't mind. Rose was in the early stages of Alzheimer's, so Marie felt as though she'd better get there early just to make sure everything was alright in the house.

At the usual time, half eight, out of force of habit, she visited the florist's just as they were opening and bought a bouquet of flowers for Rose. Ironically, she hadn't asked for any roses. Marie put the flowers on the passenger seat of the car and drove slowly to the estate where Rose lived. Parking in front of the large house and making sure she wasn't blocking the drive, she took the bouquet and walked up to the door. She didn't have her own key for Rose's house, so she rang the bell. For a moment she waited, listening to the spring breeze move the chimes that were hung on the porch. The large oak tree in the front garden whooshed in the wind, leaves bright green with the sun peeking through the branches at Marie. A minute passed by. Then another. She tried the bell again, listening this time to see if she could hear Rose coming. The house was completely silent. A familiar dreadful feeling came over her. Maybe Rose had fallen or something …

She left the porch and went to the sitting room window, cupping her hand to the glass to peak in past her reflection. In the lavishly furnished sitting room she saw no one, so she looked past through the sliding glass doors to the dining room with the large mahogany table with its chairs pushed in.

Rose was sitting in one of them, with her back to the window.

She was sitting with the newspaper open in front of her on the table and appeared to be reading it. Marie knocked on the glass hard to try to get Rose's attention, but she didn't turn around. Marie's knees suddenly felt very weak, and she almost dropped the bouquet on her way back to the porch. Looking under the mat for a key, she was partially relieved to find one.

With trembling fingers, she inserted it into the lock and let herself into the house.

COPPER RED RAIN

I lay in the field on the hot summer day, staring up at the clouds, the grass dry and wilted beneath me. Temperatures were about thirty degrees most days during this heatwave without a single drop of rain. The blue sky with white fluffy clouds drifting across with the gentle cool breeze was therapeutic to say the least. I put my arms behind my head and closed my eyes, feeling like I could fall asleep under the sun. Behind me, my house was all open windows and music playing while my mother washed the floors. Honestly, I didn't know how she managed that task in this heat. Earlier in the day she'd stepped out just to refill the bird feeders but there wasn't a winged animal in sight. She and I jokingly expressed that the birds had probably dropped dead out of the sky in this heat.

In my doze, I was listening to the distant neighing of horses in the field across the road from me, the occasional buzz of bees or the flutter of cabbage butterflies past my face. The sweet smell of honeysuckle came to my nostrils but was gone just as quickly. As I was falling asleep, I heard an awful squawk from a bird overhead. In the countryside, one gets used to the sounds that the animals living beside them make every day, but I knew that sound the split second I heard it.

It meant danger.

Sitting up and shielding my eyes from the sun, I saw a flock of seagulls, crows, ravens, hawks, eagles, finches, robins and sparrows flying inland away from the village and the sea. And it wasn't just the birds. Across the road, the cows had begun to move, the horses were running, jumping the fences. In the field far below me, across the blanket of countryside land, a large flock of sheep were merging together to flee from something unknown to my human senses.

A dreadful thought occurred to me. Animals will retreat from the sea if they sense a tsunami coming. Looking down towards the water at the seafront, I saw the crystal-clear blue shining and shimmering in the sunlight as it was just this morning and the day before and the day before that.

But then something else registered. From my vantage point, I could see the tide was going out. As I was looking at it. Like someone pulling back a carpet to reveal the sand underneath, the water receded away, to reveal the algae-covered rocks. I didn't even think about what I was doing or the consequences of my actions before I ran down to the end of the field and out onto the road to rush down to the seafront to get a better picture of this anomaly.

I wasn't the only one that saw it either, which

meant I wasn't hallucinating. Dozens of other people, local and tourist alike had gathered at the wall that bordered the rock armour on the beach preventing the waves from eroding the land anymore. Except that there wasn't any waves to erode anything, because there was no sea. All that greeted my eyes when I arrived was the dessert of wet, dark sand that stretched off towards the horizon. Not a drop of water left in sight and in its wake, dotted across the new beach, were the flailing bodies of dolphins and porpoises, and far out, one large whale now stranded and dying. Other smaller fish lay scattered across the sand too, most of them flopping around as they died. A man standing beside me held a dripping ice-cream that ran down his fingers and onto the ground, but he didn't seem to notice in the slightest.

Someone, in all the confusion and panic, must have rang the police, not knowing what else to do. When they saw what had happened, they tried to keep themselves composed and professional, ordering everyone to clear out. Not having any choice in the matter, I went home to Mum, looking out the window at the place where the Atlantic used to be.

'Terri, what's happening down there?' She asked me. Our cat Oreo was howling, running up and down the hall, fur standing up like the bristles on a brush. He was hissing out at the direction of the sea, growling and cowering down low. Mum tried petting him, but he jumped and flew outside.

That evening, when Dad came home from work, he was sweating and flustered, saying that there were reports all over the country about animals going crazy, panicking and fleeing from the coastline counties as though there was some sort of massive threat at hand. And when he switched on the television to show us, there was live coverage on several stations showing us the beaches in the different counties around the world, all as dry as a bone since the tide had retreated away to the horizon and so far, showed no signs of coming back. There was talk of sending out teams to investigate as soon as tomorrow morning. For now, they would monitor the beaches and watch for any changes in water levels until they could determine the cause of this strange event.

I went to bed that night, lying on my side, facing the curtains, listening to the yowling of Oreo outside in the garden, screeching at something unknown. My stomach twisted into a tight knot and refused to loosen for the entire night. Eventually fatigue overtook me, and I passed out for a few hours.

When I awoke, it was barely light outside and when I glanced at the clock on my nightstand, I saw that it was eleven in the morning. In the conservatory, I saw that the world outside had changed overnight, and it was darker. Where there had been a sunny day with blue skies and white clouds, now there was a blanket of black clouds covering the heavens. It hung so low that even the streetlights were still on, the sea had not returned either, but the sand was darker in composition because of the shadows cast down from overhead. When I stepped outside and felt the humid air press down on me, dread spread through my insides.

When I had washed and dressed myself, I walked down slowly to the seafront out of terror and curiosity eating away inside me. The police cars and flood lights were set up, but the public were littering the place, some of the officers were trying to tell people to go home and stay back, that everything was under control. As I approached the barricades set up to keep people back, a droplet hit me on the bridge of my nose, making me flinch. Reaching up to wipe it, it came away on my fingertips and I realised it was reddish brown in colour. It had a wet coppery smell to it like blood and faeces.

More droplets hit my head and face and then before I knew it, the sky had opened and begun to pour. The copper-coloured raindrops soaked into my clothes and my hair, staining my skin and everyone around me began to yell. People shaking their heads and pulling up their hoods once the smell registered. The police began to shout at people to get indoors, clearly entering a panicked state now. The crowd of people, as well as myself, turned to leave when the ground beneath me shook like an earthquake had begun. But then it stopped immediately. And then started again. And stopped. And started. And then I realised its rhythm was like footfalls. Giant ones that rumbled through the concrete I was standing on.

The vibrations that shook the earth were coming from behind me. Turning around to face the sand, I noticed them. On the horizon, far away and a little bit difficult to see because of the darkness of the clouds, human shaped figures were coming towards us. Like giants walking across the sands. From far away, they were indistinguishable from each other, but the closer they got, the larger they got, and I started to see their faces more clearly. They were giants, humanoid in shape but as tall as five or six storey buildings, stomping their way across the sand where the sea water was yesterday and directly towards us. They broke away from the line they walked in, and I saw that there were more of them behind the first line. Rows and rows of giants walking towards us across the beach. And that's when I saw their faces and my heart skipped a beat. One of them looked exactly like me, peeking its head out over the shoulder of the others, staring directly at me, grinning. It had the exact same teeth and eye-crinkle as me, exact same hair colour. The only difference was that it was completely naked just like all the others. Their bodies were undeniably human, bearing all the normal human anatomy. When they reached the rocks, they didn't hesitate to climb onto the pavement and that's when the giant that looked identical to me opened its mouth and showed me the inside which was dark pink and looked as though it could swallow a car with ease. I felt my knees shake but my heart pounded, adrenaline coursing through me, something telling me to turn around and run. One of the giants that stood next to mine raised its foot and brought it down on the police officer that it bore an uncanny resemblance to, crushing him flat into the ground.

I turned around and began to run and so did everyone else. It didn't matter where I was going, all I knew was that I needed to get away from those giants as fast as I possibly could. Something behind me boomed against the earth, the sound of squealing bending metal clawed at my eardrums and made me scream. Then there came the sounds of yelling, agonising cries for help, for mercy. All I saw was the ground in front of me as I sprinted forward, the world passing by in a blur as the chaos unfolded behind me. For just an instant, I turned to look, seeing the giant that looked just like me swoop down and with one arm, knock the fleeing crowd of humans to one side, sending some head-first into the surfing shop window. Then it turned to grin at me before straightening up and coming after me slowly through the brownish-red downpour that soaked the earth around me. Up ahead of me, a bunch of people were cramming themselves into a red jeep, screaming and pushing to try and get in first. Seeing my opportunity, I sprinted forwards and caught the door as they were closing it, yanking it back open.

'Let me in!' I pushed past, as they made feeble attempts to stop me. One woman attempted to block my entrance with her arms, but I knocked them aside and clambered into the seat. Not bothering with a seatbelt. They started the engine and sped out of the car park, wipers on full to clear the rain from the glass. With the boom of the giants' footsteps behind us, we drove away up the village road and inland. Turning in my seat to catch a glimpse of behind us, I saw my giantess grin down at me through the deluge, in through the rear-view window of the car and straight into my eyes, red-soaked face grotesque and distorted and uncanny to my own. Then suddenly she leapt up into the clouds and vanished from sight for a moment before coming crashing back down in the road right in front of us. The driver of the jeep slammed on the brakes, hurling me forward because I was not strapped in. The gear stick stuck into my ribs. The awful stench of faeces and blood filled my nose from how wet we all were. I retched. Looking up, my giant counterpart swung her arm back and brought it in, full force to the driver's side of the car. The door dented inwards, the glass windows shattering, and the driver's head split open.

I felt the car leave the ground and we were launched sideways through the air. Out the window, the rain was falling horizontally for a split second before the jeep whacks something, a telephone pole and I'm thrown like a ragdoll out the passenger window headfirst and onto the grass of someone's back garden.

I landed on my back, feeling it snap and then all feeling goes away. No pain or anything. I still have my eyes open and the last thing I see is the dark clouded sky, with heavy copper red rain-coloured drops hitting my face and body. My vision becomes blurry and then everything goes black.

BULLETS

The sky is dark and overcast, the day bleak and dull. What is life? I sit here in English looking out the window at the clouds that hang dangerously low. I am thinking about how they might just come down so low they would engulf the school and when you look out the window, all you would see is grey.

Fifty shades of grey. I think. Ha, I want to read that book, the trailer looked good. I might go see it. Imagine the people in the cinema start getting turned on by it all. Wouldn't be the first time, I'm sure.

Our teacher, Mr Grey, (pure coincidence) stands at the front of the class. He wears his usual tweed jacket, dark press pants, squeaky brown shoes and... oh look it's started to rain. I get distracted so easily. I sigh quietly to myself and go back to thinking about the dark clouds engulfing the school. It creeps inside, like in Stephan King's *The Mist*. Touching everyone, burning us all. Everyone breaks out in red shiny blisters that explode and produce green slimy...whatever...everyone dies. Lovely thoughts for a fifteen-year-old transition year student.

Mr Grey steps out for a moment, something tells me he needs the loo, probably the way he rushes out and into the staff room.

Please take this down class, I just have some explosive diarrhoea I need to take care of.

I try not to laugh. I amuse myself, how sad is that? So sad. How sad? So sad!

The bell rings before Mr Grey gets back and can give us homework. Good for us. To be honest I don't mind doing homework, because we're in Transition Year. *Because we get fuck all, that's why, pardon my French. I didn't know that the F word was French, wonder what it means?*

Irish is boring. Sure who am I telling? I'm good at it but it's too much of an effort to participate. Besides, the teacher is talking to himself (half the class is asleep).

Our Irish teacher Mr. Connors tries his best. Last year he gave us some helpful advice on what to do in the Junior Cert. It worked, I got a B. Other people who are too lazy to try, got D's.

To hell with them. None of the people in my Irish class, bar one or two, are my friends. I don't care about them. If they were on fire and I had a fire hose. I'd drop it. Then run away. Because 'fire bad'. I can hear shouting in the hall. Most of the boys in the class talk out of turn, throw things at each other, laugh at inappropriate things, bully other students, smoke at lunch (sometimes weed), listen to music in class, don't bring their books etc. The list goes on.

I really don't care about them. The girls just put their heads down and sleep. Most of them are bitches. Their hair colour, jewellery, tone of voice, walk, and behaviour all screams *Bitch*. I don't know what my identity would scream. *Outcast, weird, antisocial.* Whatever.

This class cannot go any slower. I'm starting to fall asleep; my back is itchy and I'm cold because some gobshite opened the window saying he was hot. It's September and it feels like Summer.

And I met you in the summer, we fell in love as the leaves turned brown.

I like that song by Calvin Harris. Again I sigh. I'm trying not to let my head smash against the desk. Because that would be unpleasant. Finally the bell rings. Thank God. I exit the room and start towards the main stairs to go up to Science. On my way up the hall to science someone grabs my shoulders. I turn around, it's Kyle.

'Hi.' I say.

'I'm signing out.' He says grinning.

'Lucky you.' I say. 'Who's collecting you?'

He shrugs.

'You haven't arranged it have you?' I say. We walk up towards the office.

'Em, yeah, I just couldn't be bothered going to the last three classes.' He says looking at his phone. He texts his Dad as we walk, saying he is sick...yeah "sick" know what I mean?

'Okay, sure I'll see you tomorrow so.' I say walking upstairs.

He looks back down at his phone. 'Have fun in science."He calls after me sarcastically. I flip him off. I just remembered that I need to finish my art project.

Our science teacher, Mrs Weasels (I know, such a name) is commonly referred to as "Froth" by us because she foams around the edge of her mouth when she talks, and also has a slight lisp. Just hope she doesn't put you near the front.

Attention on board, the first five rows will get wet. Please keep your hands and feet inside the desk at all times.

I try to concentrate on what she is saying, but it's like watching a DVD that keeps sticking. She is a lost cause. Half the class is empty and I'm bored. Some people at the back put their heads down and go to sleep. As usual. When the teacher calls out Kyle's name, I say he's gone home. This is nice, isn't it? Depressing weather, people going home every five minutes and the remaining ones are all half dead.

Class finally ends and lunch time begins. Yay! I walk down towards the lockers. People are in the way. I put my bag down and take out my sandwiches. I sit down beside Rita. She smiles at me.

'Hey.' I say.

'How was science?' She asks.

'Boring, where were you for it?' I ask.

'At the office, trying to get them to let me sign out.' She says.

'Oh not you too,' I groan. She nods and laughs.

I sigh. 'Everyone is signing out today.'

'Yeah, that's why I'm doing it. Because everyone else is gone.'

'I might sign out later. I'll see.' I say.

She stands up to get her bag.

Everyone else goes off downstairs to the canteen. Leaving certs are allowed to go off school grounds for lunch. Lucky bastards.

The locker area is empty. I copy the homework that I forgot to write down from Rita's journal. She goes over to her locker to get something. I eat the rest of my lunch. I remember my art project was due today and go wandering the halls for my art teacher Mr Freeman. Hang on, the canteen is open. *I could really go for a cookie right now. How much are they?* Reality check, canteen plus money equals food. The school food is actually okay. I take my stroll past the staff room just as Mr Freeman comes out.

'Oh, sir!' I say just as he walks past.

'Yes, Jesse.' He says pleasantly.

'You know how I'm supposed to have my art project in today? Well I haven't finished mine yet, so can I go up and finish it now if it's okay with you.'

'Of course you can. I've had a couple other people ask me the same thing. I'm headed up there now so why don't you follow me up?'

I nod.

He nods back and gives me a thumbs up. I continue my way off to the canteen. *That was a coincidence wasn't it. Now I can finish my art and turn it in on time. Good boy Jesse, roll over Jesse, sit Jesse.* My brain is talking to itself. I need to get a life. Big time. I take a look at what is for sale today. The cookies are all gone. Damn. I take a muffin instead. Close enough. I think I need to take a shower. I trot back up to the lockers, all the while thinking about my art and how I should finish it.

I brought in some turkey bones that I was thinking about gluing together as firewood, then cutting out some cardboard and making them look like people sitting around a campfire. But then I thought about making a cardboard cut-out of a ghost and having it hover over the wood. Mr Freeman said I could get a C. That's good enough for me.

Ha that rhymes, maybe later I could-

Somebody screams downstairs and I hear something that sounds like fireworks going off down by the canteen. Then lots more screaming. I pause, listening for more. Then someone comes running up the stairs and around the corner. They have blood all over their jumper. I recognise him from the year above me. His name is George. Blood spills from his abdomen. I cover my mouth to stop myself from screaming. More footsteps up the stairs.

I realise that those "fireworks" I heard a few moments ago were not fireworks at all. Someone has a gun, there are people in the school with guns. I see someone's shadow on the wall and dive to my right to hide behind the wall. The door to the prayer room is right beside me. I open in and emerge into the musty dark room. The blinds are open. I close the door over until only a crack is left. Then I look out the window. George is now on the floor face down. I think he is dead.

More people come up the stairs. Two men (at least I think they are men) dressed in something that looks like army uniforms carrying semi-automatic Uzis. I duck down and hold my breath. They pass by and disappear around the corner down the hall. I take a deep breath and stand up. I'm shaking.

I have to get out of here. Like now, oh God where

do I go. I exit the room and peek around the corner. The two-armed gunmen have vanished. What is happening here? Why are people shooting at us? My brain has a million questions all at once.

Breath Jesse, just keep your head and think. Find the nearest exit.

I shake my head. Now is the time for running, this is like those night terrors that I used to get as a child. I can see down the stairs, there is someone lying face down on the ground, it's a girl, her hair covers her face, her hands, bloody. Oh God, please let there be a way out of this. I want to burst into tears. But I can do that after I've gotten out of here. I creep down the stairs, two students are lying on the floor. The girl, and one of the other seniors who's a prefect, I've seen him around. His face, chest and legs all have numerous holes in them. I peer over the banisters. More bodies, some streaks of blood, a classroom door is left open. I go back up. I have to leave now, who knows where those guys in the uniform have gone.

Maybe some people have already gotten out. Leaving Certs who left will be okay. People outside might have fled. I go down one hall to the windows. I can't see anyone outside. But there might be.

More gunfire. I bite my lip. Think Jesse, think. Okay, well if they are downstairs then I could climb out a window. No, find an exit. Oh!

I remember there are fire exits down at the other end of the hall. Bingo! They are down beside the science rooms. They lead down two flights of stairs and to the back and front of the building. Once on the ground you just run through the back or front gate. The back gate goes up by the shop, the front leads up the big drive out in the open car park. I think one of the back-fire escapes is my best bet.

I can't resist, I sprint down the hall, towards the classrooms. They are near the front of the buildings. Gunfire rings out somewhere nearby upstairs. Flight is essential at this point. I can see the doors, getting closer. I can almost taste the fresh air. Yes, come on, my legs won't move fast enough. Keep running.

Just keep running, just keep running, reminds me of-

As I reach the end of the hallway, I see someone coming up the stairs. It's one of those armed men with guns blocking me off. Oh shit.

He turns towards me and points the gun. I don't have time to scream. A burning pain tears through my abdomen. My hands fly down to my stomach. I look down to see blood seeping through my white cotton shirt. It stains my watch, and I feel faint as my knees buckle. I hit the deck as the man in the uniform approaches me.

My vision blurs and I can't hear anything except my own pounding heart that is now slowing down as my head smacks against the floor. Everything goes dark very slowly and then nothing more.

VINCENT

Vincent and I sat in the ice cream parlour in silence for about half an hour, while I periodically fed him his banana split. He would open his mouth when I raised the spoon and chew lazily. I tried to swallow the lump in my throat and remained thankful he couldn't see me if I cried. A few times he reached up to slip his finger beneath the bandage covering his eyes, scratching an itch, I presumed.

'Is it too tight?' I said, leaning forward.

'No. It's okay.' He said, barely audible. He let his hand fall back into his lap and the lump in my throat got bigger.

'I have to go to the bathroom.' He announced, reaching for his walking stick before I could get it. He pushed himself out of the booth and didn't wait for me to grip his arm and guide him to the restroom. For a moment, I considered letting him go alone, but decided it was a bad idea and rushed after him, not caring if the waitress cleared our table. Vince wasn't eating anyway, and I didn't particularly like bananas. I touched him lightly on the shoulder as he went down the small ramp, leading to the main part of the parlour. 'Wait for me, please.'

He said nothing as we went into the men's room. I almost went into the stall with him, but he closed the door before I could. I waited, avoiding my reflection in the mirror while I blew my nose with some blue tissue paper and tried to keep up a brave face for when we went back outside. He didn't urinate on himself this time, and actually managed to wash his hands properly, holding them under the dryer before taking off out the door without me. Again.

'Where would you like to go now?' I asked, trying to sound interested and happy, but calm at the same time. We were leaving the ice-cream parlour and crossing the deserted village road to go over to the ramp and walk down to the beach. Vince tripped on the curb and stumbled forward. I instinctively put my arms out to grab him, but he steadied himself. Blushing, he walked slower this time, not pulling away when I slid my arm around the crook of his elbow. Together, our steps almost in perfect synchronisation, we descended the wooden slope towards the sands. The pink and orange sky glowed brightly as the sun dipped below the horizon. The salty air was a welcome change from the warm city smog I'd been breathing in for the last eight months. That June evening was perfect. Well … almost.

Vincent didn't say anything as we walked across the beach, encountering no one at that point in the evening. He had barely spoken to me since I arrived. When I called his home to take him out that evening, I received a hug from his mother and a firm, warm handshake from his father. He still didn't say anything during the taxi ride down to the seafront or when we sat down in the ice-cream parlour. Ghosts of memories crept up and threatened to burst into my mind, recalling old conversations and events that seemed like they were a dream at this point. And during that walk I wondered if the same memories were in his head, if he wanted to talk about them? Across the water, the sun disappeared, and a cool breeze sprung up. I wanted to stop and admire the purple sky, but didn't, because I had to remind myself that Vincent wouldn't be able to see it.

'Is it gone? …The sun.' He asked, abruptly.

I had to clear my throat to get my voice to come back. 'Yes.'

'Okay.'

For just a moment, I wanted to describe it, but I couldn't find the right words.

'What colour are the clouds?' He asked me then.

'Purple, with a tint of orange around their edges. Like in your paintings. The one you gave me for my birthday.'

I thought I saw a glimpse of a smirk on his lips, but it was gone before I could take it in properly.

'Can we talk?' I asked.

'Isn't that what we're doing?'

'I mean about the accident. It might help. If you're comfortable with that.'

He swallowed hard and hung his head. 'Michael, you don't want to know that. That's not what I want this to be about. Can we just pretend it's one of our old walks on the beach.'

'I'd like for us to talk about it. It would help lift this weight off my shoulders. I feel like I'm walking on eggshells around you. I don't want to do that. That's not what I came home for. And I know that's not what you want either.'

He wet his lips and looked directly at me without seeing me. 'I lost my eyesight in the accident. That's all there is to it. Now I can't see your face, or my own, or paint or do anything that I used to. This is my life now. Maybe it would have been better if I had died instead.'

'No it wouldn't.' I said, even though I could see where he was coming from. I might have thought the same thing if it were me in his place. So, my job was to comfort and reassure him that it wasn't meant to be like that. That we still had each other. That I wasn't going anywhere.

'I love you.' I said, lost for words beyond that.

For a moment, he didn't answer, then I saw a smile lift the corners of his lips just slightly. A woman with two Labradors walked by, the two of them panting and wagging their tails.

'Do you mean it?' He whispered to me.

I wrapped my arms around him and hugged him tightly. 'Always.'

He clung to me. 'I was afraid that you wouldn't feel the same way. That you'd be scared of me because of this.'

'Never.'

I was, at first. When I got the news, away at school, I was terrified that when I came home to visit him, he would look grotesque, nothing at all like the boy I fell in love with two and a half years prior. But with the bandages over his eyes, he looked exactly the same, apart from the cast and sling his arm was in at the time. But once they'd taken that off, the old Vince returned. All that was missing was his blue eyes. A sight I was afraid I would forget as time went on. Even now, I can't quite see them as clearly in my mind's eye, as ironic as that sounds.

When we had finished our walk, we caught a taxi back out to his house and this time, he held my hand firmly with both of his, his head dropped forward, probably disappointed that he couldn't enjoy looking out the window with me. When we arrived outside his house and I got out of the car, dashing around to his side to help him out, we went inside and upstairs to his room without speaking to his parents. The two of them were sitting out the back, sipping their glasses of wine and chatting constantly from the sounds of it. In the upstairs bathroom, he beckoned for me to follow him in and pushed the door closed, setting his stick leaning against the sink counter.

'I want you to see me.' He said, nervously.

'I beg your pardon?' I said, even though I already had an idea what he was getting at.

'I want you to change my bandages.' He said, trying to keep his voice calm. I was glad he couldn't see me then, for he would have seen the panic on my face, or the colour drain from it.

'Vincent. Are you sure?'

'…Yes.'

He stood there for a moment, unmoving. I stood up, wiping my hands on my trousers. 'Okay … where are they? The bandages?'

'In the cabinet underneath the sink. On the left.'

I took them out and placed them on the counter gently, also picking out the cotton wool. 'Do I need to wrap the wool over your eyes?'

He smirked. 'You can't fool me. Besides, I don't have any, remember.'

'Okay, smart arse. You'll have to walk me through it. I'm no state nurse, so get ready to scream for your Mum if I hurt you.'

'I'll have to jab out your eyes if you do.'

'Then we can be blind together.' I said, to which

neither of us laughed. But the whiff of humour was in the air between us and that was a step forward from earlier at least. I kept the materials beside me as I reached up around his right temple to unstick the bandage and begin to unwind them, my heart rate quickening. I braced myself for the sight I was about to behold, kicking myself for another pun I'd inadvertently made. When the bandage fell away, the cotton wool began to as well, traces of congealed blood with it as the wound stared at me in full view.

It was deep red around where his eyes should have been, I could see both his sockets, and the missing cartilage from where the accident had destroyed the bridge of his nose. If I were to press on it, it would flatten down completely. I wondered if it felt weird, having the air whirling around inside your sockets like that. If it was refreshing or annoying. I resisted the urge to reach up and touch them, for fear that would hurt him, which was, of course, the last thing I wanted.

'How does it look?' He asked. Just seeing him speak with those holes in his face was making me squirm and feel itchy.

'It's horrible.' I said, honestly. 'You look frightening like that.' My voice trembled.

'I guess I won't need to dress up for Halloween this year.' He said, smirking again.

I gritted my teeth as I felt my eyes burn with tears that needed to fall. Despite that, I picked up the cotton wool and began to carefully administer the new bandages to Vincent's face. He stood still, trusting me with all of it. When his sockets were covered, he reached up tentatively to take my cheeks in his hands and leaned down to kiss me, gently. I let him, feeling the bandage rub against my nose. His lips tasted the exact same and I was glad of that. Something familiar, that hadn't been altered or destroyed. We embraced each other and let the seconds pass by inside the bathroom silently. The light above our heads hummed with electricity. After a while, we broke apart and I put the rest of the bandages back. I followed him into his room, and we sat down on his bed. He reached for his tablet and handed me the earphones. 'Plug these in.' He said.

'What are we listening to?'

'A radio play.'

While the summer evening came to a close and the sky darkened outside, we sat in the comfort of his bedroom, his head leaning on my shoulder. I closed my eyes and just listened to the sound of the voices whispering in my ear and the heat of his body at my side.

ALL I HAVE FOR YOU IS CONTEMPT

Zara moved in with us in October of five years ago. She and my Dad hit it off straight away, but I never liked her. I couldn't put my finger on it, there was just something about her that rubbed me the wrong way. Maybe it had something to do with the fact that she and I had very similar names. My name is Sarah, hers is Zara. I thought that was kind of creepy. To add to that, she always had a habit of 'borrowing' my clothes without my permission, which really pissed me off. I never grew to love her, or even tolerate her. I avoided her whenever I could.

So, when the police came to our house this morning to tell us that Zara had been killed in a bank robbery gone wrong, I had to bite the inside of my cheek to stop myself from smiling.

That might seem like a cruel thing to do, smile upon finding out that she was dead, but I couldn't help it. I cover my mouth with my hand and run to my room, making it look like I am devastated, but really, I am relieved. It suddenly feels like a huge weight has slipped away from my shoulders. I sit on my bed and look up at my Velux window in the ceiling at the blue sky with its fluffy white clouds drifting by. I glance at my reflection in the mirror on my desk, seeing my face, colourful and bright, staring back at me, framed by mousy brown hair. I get up and tie it back with a clip in order to see my face better, wipe my eyes and go downstairs again. The police are gone, and Dad is standing there, staring at the carpet. After a moment he looks up at me, lost.

'They want me to go down and identify the body.' He says.

'I'll come with you.' I say, not wanting him to have to go through it alone.

'You don't have to, pet. I can do it myself.' He says, his brow furrowing.

'Not gonna happen. I need to see it for myself.' I say, going to get my jacket.

At the morgue, they only lift the sheet past her face, and I can see that she looks fine. It's intact, albeit paler because she's dead. I had visions of half her head missing from being shot, like they'd said. But apparently, she had taken two bullets to the chest. Of course, they wouldn't show us that. I take a moment to look at her one last time, her chubby face, without her purple-rimmed glasses on, her short brown hair, double chin and thick shoulders. Even in death, she manages to disgust me.

When we go home, Dad says he isn't feeling well and is going to bed. I hung up his jacket for him.

'Do you want me to get you anything?' I ask as he reaches the top of the stairs.

He shakes his head.

'Will I heat up your hot water bottle?'

He hesitates for a moment before nodding. 'Yeah, okay.'

I lean against the counter in the kitchen, staring out the window into the back garden. My reflection stares back at me, eyes hard and cold, no sign of tears in them at all now. It feels strange … I keep thinking that I'm supposed to feel sad. I take the beaded hot water bottle out of the microwave and bring it upstairs to Dad before I go to my room.

Lying on the bed with my headphones on, I hug one of my pillows tightly. Music fills the void in my head, drowning out Zara's lingering voice from this morning. She came into my room, smiling like a hyena at me in bed and said that she was going to the bank to withdraw some money. I grinded my teeth and bit down on my bed clothes as I heard her close the front door behind her, not knowing that it would be the last time she would.

Music always helps me sleep and drown out the world around me. Call it a coping mechanism if you want. I close my eyes and let the rhythm and beat wash over me as I doze off. Zara's smiling face swims behind my eyelids, thin lips stretching over tiny teeth, double chins folding over onto each other, purple glasses over beady brown eyes that squint down at me malevolently …

'Sarah,' Dad's voice wakes me from my slumber. I lift my head and take off the headphones, wiping the sleep from my eye lashes.

'What time is it?' I ask.

'It's a little after seven. I'm gonna order a take-away for dinner. Are you okay with that?'

'Sure.' I say, sitting up. 'How are you feeling now?'

'Better. I think the rest helped.' He says, standing back up and kissing me on the top of my head.

While we wait for the take-away to arrive, Dad switches on the television to fill up the silence that presses between us. He steps out into the hall to ring someone. I overhear his conversation and it seems to be with the staff from the morgue. He informs them that he doesn't want a funeral. I can tell that the person on the other end of the phone didn't expect that because he has to repeat himself.

'I'm not paying for a memorial service. I don't want one. Do what you want with her.' The doorbell rings. 'I'm sorry, but I have to go. I have other matters that need attending to.' He hangs up.

While we're eating, his phone rings and he snatches it up, half-expecting it to be the morgue again. But it's not, from the sounds of it. He steps out of the room for a moment, then comes back in, the conversation having already ended.

'There's somebody coming to speak to us tomorrow about Zara.'

'Is it the police?' I ask.

'No. It's a reporter. Somebody named Allison.'

'Oh.' I say. 'That'll be fun.'

Dad gives me a look and I see the worry behind it. He sits down beside me at the island and absent-mindedly picks at his chips. I reach across and take his hand. 'It's okay now. She can't hurt either of us anymore.'

He squeezes my knuckles before letting go. 'I'm not worried about that. I'm worried about this reporter and what she'll ask us.'

Allison, it turns out, is a tall woman of Asian ethnicity, with long wavy black hair and a beige trench jacket and heels. She carries herself into our home with an air of business and professionality that I've never quite seen in a person before.

Dad shakes her hand and then introduces me to her.

'Can I get you anything Allison?' I ask. 'Tea, coffee, water?'

'Some coffee would be lovely please, Sarah.' She says.

When the three of us are sitting down in the kitchen, she offers us her condolences and then asks us about Zara. She also asks for our permission to record the conversation. Dad and I exchange a glance before we both say yes.

'How long has she lived here with you?' Allison asks.

'Five years. Well, it would have been five in October.' Says Dad.

'And in all that time, you only stayed 'boyfriend-girlfriend'?'

'Yes. She never seemed interested in taking it any further.'

'And yet she wanted to move in with you.' Allison says, tilting her head.

Dad wets his lips and looks at her. 'I didn't want to take it further either.' He confesses.

'And why is that?'

'Because she wasn't the type of woman that would make a good wife. She never brought up marriage or anything. Just seemed happy to live under the same roof as Sarah and myself.'

'Why do you think that is?' She asks. 'What made you think she wouldn't make a good wife?'

'She wasn't a good person.' I say. That seems to peak Allison's interest. She nods for me to continue. I swallow, looking at Dad, who seems quite nervous, probably guessing what I'm about to say.

Now is the time to be honest about it.

People should know what kind of person Zara was. Besides, this'll be my way of getting back at her, by dragging her name through the mud. And honestly, that kind of makes me glad.

'Zara seemed eager to move in with us right from the beginning. Which, I thought was kind of strange, y'know?' I say. 'Something about her just got under my skin. But she seemed so bubbly and happy all the time. It was like she was breaking down our front door to get in here to see what we were doing. How we were living. It wasn't long before I realised why she was that way. She always wanted to drive me to school, pick me up, help me with my homework, and bring me shopping. She went everywhere with us. She never let Dad and I do anything on our own. She would always worm her way into whatever we were doing.'

Allison is drinking in everything I am saying.

'Even matters that didn't concern her, like legal stuff, financial stuff, she would always go with Dad to deal with it. That always pissed me off. She came to my parent-teacher meetings too. And she wasn't my legal guardian. I thought it was strange. And so did Dad.'

'She insisted we have a joint bank account.' Says Dad.

'It had to go her way or no way. She didn't take no for an answer. If you disagreed, you'd pay for it. And *boy*, did we pay for it.' I say.

Allison checks the recorder to make sure it's still getting all of this, then nods for me to continue, calmly sipping her coffee.

'She poisoned Dad's food once.' I say, hearing the venom behind it. 'She was crushing up slug pellets and putting them in with his mashed potato. I had to ring an ambulance to bring him to the hospital to have his stomach pumped.' My lip starts to tremble, recalling the memory.

At fifteen years old, I came home from school one afternoon after basketball practice. I was drenched in sweat, thirsty for a drink of cool water and wanted nothing more than to have a nice hot shower. I couldn't find Dad anywhere until I went into his room and found him lying face down in a puddle of his own vomit. He had tried to get the slug pellets out of his system by sticking his fingers down his own throat, but it didn't work. At that age, finding your Dad in such a state and having to try and keep my voice coherent on the phone to the paramedic, calmly telling me to give her my address while Dad was dying beside me …

'Did you tell someone?' Allison asks.

'We couldn't prove it. I mean, we never caught her red-handed, like. So, it would have looked like we were just pointing fingers.' I say.

'She made sure to cover her tracks. She was very good at that.' Dad says, darkly.

'She withdrew a load of money from our bank account and spent it behind Dad's back. There was nothing she couldn't get away with.'

Allison has a glint in her eyes after all of this. She drinks the last of her coffee before she asks me one last question. 'Do you think she got what she deserved, Sarah?'

I don't need to hesitate or think before I answer. 'Yes.'

Allison thanks us for our time and tells us to keep an eye out for the next issue of the paper. When it's printed, I pick up a copy of it at the shop and sit down to read through it. Allison does her homework it seems, because the article has a whole biography about Zara, filling me in on the woman I've spent the last five years putting up with in the same house. The article mentions all, from Zara's parents saying she was everything they could have asked for in a daughter to them giving her everything she ever wanted, to sending her to college across the country because she said it would make her dreams come true. It mentions how she was brought to the small claims court so many times, she was on a nearly first name basis with the judge there.

The second half of the article sheds new light on Zara. According to what Allison found out, She wasn't a stranger to the law, by any means. She was brought to court for shoplifting, several times in Dublin. She was wanted up north in Belfast for writing bad cheques. Of course, up there, it's a different jurisdiction, so there was nothing they could do to her once she'd crossed the border and came back to the Republic. She stole money from people she'd been in relationships with in the past. They've even included one of her mug shots in the paper. Then it mentions her life with Dad and I. How she weaselled her way into our house and stayed hidden under our roof for almost five years. Allison even went ahead and recounted my tale of Dad being poisoned by slug pellets.

Lastly the article mentions the bank robbery that went askew, with the men in their balaclavas grabbing Zara and her trying to fight back, only to receive two bullets to the chest for all her troubles. They caught the three robbers a few hours after they escaped the bank. They're now in custody awaiting trial.

I let Dad read through the paper when I brought it home. The cashier at the shop said quietly to me that he was sorry for my loss. I simply said; 'Thank you' and left. What I felt like saying was 'I'm not.'

When I get home, I sit down at the island in the kitchen and stare out the window. A lot of things are going through my head right now. Most of it is about Zara and what she said to me. After the slug pellets incident, I tried to confront her about it, while Dad was recovering in hospital.

She was standing at the back door, smoking out into the winter air. She heard me come downstairs and her eyes met mine while I stood in the doorway. I remember the look she gave me; she was smug. She knew that I knew, and she also knew she'd gotten away with it. There really was no way of proving otherwise. Who would believe me? A fifteen-year-old girl at the time, pointing the finger at her stepmother for trying to poison her Dad. Please. It sounds like something from a Fairy-tale.

Cinderella, I thought. In the original ending to that story, the glass slipper fits, and Cinderella is taken to the palace to marry the prince. As the carriage takes her away, Cinderella's bird friends dive-bomb the stepmother and stepsisters, gouging their eyes out with their beaks.

'He'll be fine.' Zara said to me, finishing her cigarette. 'Nothing to worry about.' She flicked the butt into the grass and walked out of the kitchen, pinching my arm hard as she went.

Remembering this, I glare at the back door now, fighting the urge to throw something at it. Dad comes in and fills the kettle with water.

'Tea?' He asks.

'Yes, please.' I say. I can still hear the venom in my voice.

'Are you alright? You sound upset.'

'Of course I'm upset.' I say.

Dad boils the kettle and comes to stand beside me.

'Listen, it's alright. I know it's awful, what happened to her and yeah, maybe she did deserve it. But the important thing is that she's gone now. Okay? She can't hurt us anymore.'

'She almost killed you, Dad. If she had done that, what would have happened to me? Where would I have gone?'

'…I know. But I didn't die. I'm not going to die for a long time. Okay? C'mere.'

He puts his arms around me and hugs me tight. And I hug him back, closing my eyes and listening to the sound of his heartbeat and the whistle of the kettle as it boils on the cooker. With the sound of his heart beating steadily in his chest against my ear, I breathe out slowly.

It's gonna be okay now.

Zara's ashes are delivered to us in an urn the following week. It's a simple brown one with no design on it. Dad stands in the hall, holding it away at arm's length.

'What do you want to do with it?' I ask, folding my arms across my chest and leaning in the doorway to the kitchen.

'Flush them down the toilet.' He says.

'We can't do that. It'd clog the drains.'

He scoffs and shakes his head. 'Even in death, you still fuck things up around this house.'

'Give it to me here, I'll throw it in the bin.' I take the urn from him and bring it out the back door and around the side of the house to the black and blue bins parked behind the side gate. I put the urn down to open the lid, then pick it up and stare at it. I'm holding all that's left of her in my hands. Her entire existence is in my grasp right now. And honestly, it feels disgusting. I raise it up and fling it into the bin, hearing it smash open as it hits the bottom. The image from years ago, of Dad lying face down in his own spit on the bedroom floor after eating that potato that contained the crushed-up slug pellets, refuses to leave my head. I slam the lid shut.

'Fuck you, Zara.' I say to the bin, giving it a strong kick before going back inside to wash my hands.

When Dad goes to bed, I stay up late to watch some television, not really paying attention to what's happening on screen. When it gets to midnight, I turn everything off, lock up and go upstairs to my room. I lie down and put on my headphones, letting the music fill my head. This time, I'm able to tear the image of her out of my head fully. I lie on my back and close my eyes, feeling a lot more relaxed. I think confessing all of what happened to Allison has helped me. And honestly, I think that Dad and I are finally safe now, which makes me happy. I don't have to worry that she's in the next room with him, or that she might try and poison him. She's outside in the bin, where she belongs …

I turn off the music and take off my headphones, leave my room and go across the hall to Dad. I look at him from the doorway. I can see it in his face, that he's more relaxed. Seeing him alone in the bed, I feel a great tension in my neck that I wasn't too aware of begin to dissolve.

In the growing darkness of my room, I lie in bed, feeling a sense of bliss for what feels like the first time. I roll on my side and look at the photograph of mum, dad and I that I've taped to my wall from years ago.

Mum died when I was twelve. She had been diagnosed with ovarian cancer two years before that, but she never told me exactly what was wrong with her. Probably fearing that I was too young to understand. Dad told me she was sick, and we needed to take care of her. I sat with her at night time after dinner and read to her, hoping it would make her feel better. One evening, she took my hand, told me she loved me and stopped breathing. You'd think I would have called out for Dad to come or cried or something, but surprising myself, I stayed seated and held her limp fingers. Maybe I thought … Maybe I wasn't ready to let it hit me. When Dad came in to tell me it was time for bed, he realised she was gone and the rest of it happened.

Two years later, just after I turned fourteen, he brought Zara home with him. In retrospect, I think he was lonely and just wanted somebody - anybody - to have at his side. That knee-jerk reaction, if you will, led to him getting poisoned and me deciding not to leave home to go to college after finishing my exams. I could have gone away, but I never applied to anywhere. How could I? And leave him alone with her? What would happen if I came home one weekend and found out that she'd finally killed him? No, it was better that I stayed here, to make sure he was kept safe. I guess, in a weirdly dark, karmic way, the universe heard my plea …

I turn the other way in the bed, feeling heavier and warmer now. Sleep pulls me down in no time and for the first time in five years, I actually sleep soundly without anyone sneaking into my room to watch me.

In the morning, I wake up and go to the bathroom to wash my face before I hear the binmen out front emptying the rubbish. One of them unlocks our side-gate as usual and takes the bins over to the lorry. I watch as they tip them upside down, emptying Zara's ashes into it and place it back around the side, before moving onto the next house. I go back to bed. Later, when the sun has cleared the horizon, I'll go downstairs and throw out all of her photo frames and albums. I'll empty all her clothes and belongings into black rubbish bags and bring them to the clothes bank in town. I'll take the first step towards making this our house again.

ABOUT THE AUTHOR

Eoin Leydon O Connor

Eoin Leydon O Connor is a native of Sligo, Ireland. He is a qualified writer with a Bachelor of Arts in Writing & Literature. As an avid horror fan, he enjoys watching horror films, tv series, as well as reading horror novels, manga and playing video games.

Eoin has an eclectic taste in music and enjoys listening to everything from Rock to Jazz. He likes long walks and reading in his spare time.
Rural Tales is his debut collection of short stories.